NERVOUS READERS BEWARE

I am a sweet and innocent little brother,
innocent of all wrong and doer of only
good deeds . . . Some readers may be
shocked by the appalling mental and
physical torture to which I am subjected
by my big brother and sister on a daily
basis . . . But now I have the power that
comes from being a

REVENGER

THE WAR DIARIES OF ALISTAIR FURY

JAMIE RIX

Illustrated by Nigel Baines

CORGI YEARLING BOOKS

To Jonty
(or should I say Alistair?)

THE WAR DIARIES OF ALISTAIR FURY:
Bugs on the Brain
A CORGI YEARLING BOOK : 0 440 86554 9

First publication in Great Britain

PRINTING HISTORY
Corgi Yearling edition published 2002

3 5 7 9 10 8 6 4

Set in 12/14.5pt Comic Sans by
Phoenix Typesetting, Ilkley, West Yorkshire.

Corgi Books are published by Random House Children's Books,
61–63 Uxbridge Road, London W5 5SA,
a division of The Random House Group Ltd,
in Australia by Random House Australia (Pty) Ltd,
20 Alfred Street, Milsons Point, Sydney, NSW 2061, Australia,
and in New Zealand by Random House New Zealand Ltd,
18 Poland Road, Glenfield, Auckland 10, New Zealand
and in South Africa by Random House (Pty) Ltd,
Endulini, 5a Jubilee Road, Parktown 2193, South Africa.

Made and printed in Great Britain by
Cox & Wyman Ltd, Reading, Berkshire.

www.kidsatrandomhouse.co.uk

My
Daily Diary

This diary belongs to Alistair Fury
Age 11
Address 47 Atrocity Road, Tooting, England
Favourite Colour Not pink!
Favourite Boy Band Oh no, is this a drippy girl's diary?
Cuddly Teddy Bear's Name It is! That's just typical! Everything in my life is double pants with extra pongy cheese!
Person You Would Most Like to Kiss Oh perlease!
Person You Would Most Like to kill - William and Mel

Notes

I am a sweet little brother, innocent of all wrong and doer only of good deeds. Butter doesn't melt in my mouth. I am keeping this secret diary so that other little brothers in the world will know that they are not alone in being the most unloved and persecuted human life form on the planet. Is there *anybody* out there who loves us?

5

Sometimes, when poor little me is tortured by the vicious half-nelsons, dead legs and ear twists of my big brother (who's a lazy cheating liar), and the poisonous tongue and towel slaps of my big sister (who says she loves every boy in the world *except* me), I am forced to get even in any way I can. It is my hope that some of my revenge tactics might prove useful to other little brothers faced with evil brothers and sisters who are twice their size and half their intelligence!

NERVOUS READERS BEWARE

Some readers may be shocked by the appalling physical and mental torture to which I am subjected by my big brother and sister on a daily basis. Some may think me heroic and wonderful for suffering this torture without a word of complaint. Some may want to send me money or put a statue of me up in Trafalgar Square. Some may even want to liken me to Gandhi or Jesus. But if it's a toss up, just send the money, because I'm saving up for a motorbike when I'm sixteen.

ALISTAIR THE GREAT

And handsome too, if you could see me

We were in the tent in my garden.

'It's so unfair! My name is Alistair not Alice!' I cried. There were nearly tears in my eyes. My best friends, Aaron and Ralph, could see that I was suffering. We were sleeping in the Great Outdoors like wild bear trappers, only with the back door of the house open in case we needed the loo or got scared. I'd already been into the house four times. Once for blankets, once for fly spray, once for a 'spider hammer' and once for crisps. I was telling my best friends how utterly awful and tragic my life was as a little brother and they were listening and nodding in agreement.

By the way, Ralph had eaten so many chocolate biscuits that he'd been sick in a little puddle just outside the tent door.

We'd been out to have a look at it twice already, because Aaron wanted to see how quickly the flies would eat it.

'My big brother was allowed to stay out in a tent when he was *five*,' I said indignantly. 'I'm eleven and this is my first time! I mean, that's not fair, is it?'

'What about your big sister?' said Ralph.

'What *about* my big sister?' I said. 'When I was three, she was good at making pasta pictures, but otherwise I hate her. She's so boring about her beautiful new boyfriend.'

THE BEAUTIFUL NEW BOYFRIEND

His name is Luke, but Mel calls him Luke the Nuke, because she thinks he's dynamite! **Ugh!** Luke the Puke more like, because they spend all their time snogging!

Also, Mel says she wants to be an actress, but I know that's just so she can get on Mum's telly show when she knows it's *my* turn!

'You're going on telly?' gasped Aaron, when I told him that.

'William did it last year, but he's not cute anymore like me. He's got bigger and hairier and treats me like a slave! Mum said if I was well behaved for the whole next month she'd ask her producer.'

You should have seen the look of envy on my best friends' faces.

'But you'll be famous!' said Ralph.

'Yup! With my first million I'm buying a supermodel and a Ferrari Testosterone!'

'I know why they call you Alice,' said Aaron suddenly. He's never been quick off the mark. 'Maybe there was a mix-up at the hospital when you were born. Maybe the baby your mother gave birth to was a boy,

Dad will have to stop hating me now for being a sporting disappointment and love me as a daughter. I hope I don't get given embroidery to do instead of computer games.

but the baby they took home was a girl and they've never noticed!'

'You mean underneath all my dangly bits I'm really a girl?' I said.

'Question,' said Ralph. 'Did you cry at *The Ugly Duckling* first time you read it?'

'Yes,' I said, 'I did.'

'Girl,' he said.

I was stunned. I didn't want to be a girl, although it did explain why I was so bad at football.

Then suddenly I started crying. I think it was something to do with knowing that I was a boy really, so being called a girl really hurt. Anyway, as I howled like a baby Ralph called me a girl again, and the noise brought Dad rushing out of the house. He was in his underpants and hissed something about waking the neighbours and me sitting on a cushion for a week, then went back indoors.

'See,' I blubbed. 'They all pick on me.'

Ralph laughed.

'What's so funny about that?' I said. 'I'm doomed!'

'Not that,' he said. 'Your cat's just fallen off the wall.'

'That's not *my* cat,' I told him. 'It's my big sister's. Lost its tail in a cat flap, when the flap flapped back like a guillotine.' Come to think of it, that was probably when my big sister stopped liking me, because somehow the tail found itself hidden *by accident* under a lettuce leaf on her plate, and I got the blame when she nearly ate it!

I am cleverly writing 'by accident' in case this diary should fall into enemy hands. Then I cannot be blamed for anything, because 'by accident's are accidents, which are nobody's fault!

'I thought the lettuce leaf might rub the tail better like a dock leaf,' I told my grim parents when they stood me on the kitchen table and demanded an explanation. 'I thought the tail might grow another body or something!'

Mel thought it was a huge hairy caterpiller and screamed the house down. It was brilliant! 'Anyway,' I said to Ralph, 'since that day, the cat has lost its sense of balance and falls off walls all the time.' This time it had fallen on our fat dog – Mr E.

Mr E is a pug dog that belonged to my granny before she died. Everyone hates him, which means that he and me have got quite a lot in common, because everyone hates me too. He's bad tempered, horribly ugly, licks blood, his breath stinks and he wipes his nose on my socks. For some unknown reason, we saved his life. If *we* hadn't taken him after Granny's funeral, the man from the restaurant on the motorway would have chopped him up into cheeseburgers, apparently.

Suddenly there was wailing and whining outside the tent where it was dead dark and spooky. A shadow of a giant monster fell across the roof. We could see its arms and legs pressed against the canvas just like in a horror film! I screamed a high-pitched scream, and Ralph and Aaron did the same. 'Help! It's a werewolf!' I shouted. Aaron thought it was Dracula and

Ralph thought it was a dead body that had got up and walked! 'Or that Tony Blair Witch thing!' I cried. We were so scared Aaron peed on the biscuits by accident.

This was a real accident. Aaron would not pee on the biscuits 'by accident', because he loves biscuits.

Then the monster put its face through the flap and the screaming stopped. It was my big brother William. He was laughing as if it was the best joke in the world. He was laughing so hard we could see his fillings. He called us *girls*!

'I'm going to get you!' I promised.

'I'd like to see you try!' he said. So I did. It wasn't that hard actually.

'Mummy! Daddy!' I shouted. 'William's being horrible to me. He's trying to scare us to death!' That was all there was to it. I heard a door slam, then my big sister poked her head through the tent flap. Her face was covered in green mud and looked really cross.

'Some of us have got a really important date tomorrow,' she growled. 'Some of us are trying to get some beauty sleep!'

'Some of us need it!' I whispered to Aaron, but unfortunately she heard. Now it was *her* turn to hate me.

'And who said you could have

Napoleon?' she screeched.

'No, please, Mel,' I said, clutching the cat to my chest, 'he's my hot water bottle. I'm cold.' But she snatched him out of my arms and took him back in the house just so I couldn't have him. And that was when Dad turned up for a second time, sent William to his room and glared at me. 'If this is "well-behaved", I'm a pork chop,' he growled. 'Your mother is exhausted.'

'But William was trying to murder us,' I said in my most pathetic voice.

'I don't care if he was trying to flash fry you in oil of sperm whale and force feed you to flesh-stripping locusts!' he said (which was a particularly nice thing for a father to say).

'You promised your mother you'd be good, Alistair. If you carry on like this she won't have you on her show. Now start behaving like a human being and let your mother get some rest!' Dad stumbled back indoors, treading in Ralph's sick as he went. When it squidged between his toes he made more noise than all of us put together!

'Can your mum get *us* on the telly?' Ralph asked.

'Oh please,' begged Aaron.

'No,' I said. 'I can go on because I'm related. You're just ordinary people. It doesn't count.'

'Bum!' sniggered Ralph. 'If your mum's a TV cook, does that mean she cooks TVs?' Then he put on silly voices and pretended to be me and my mum talking.

'"What's for supper, famous mummy?"

"Lovely roast aerials, Alistair."'

'No,' I said sadly, 'it means she poisons us when she tries out her new recipes.'

As we were drifting off to sleep, Aaron whispered, 'Alistair, your family really *don't* love you, do they?'

'Not much,' I sobbed softly. 'But I'll make them pay!'

Then, after a long dark pause Aaron said, 'We could be your family. Ralph and me. Just a thought. Night.'

SUNDAY

Woke up at first light and could not believe my luck. It was like the Revenge Fairy had been. Only it wasn't a fairy, it was a revenge cat. Napoleon had brought a dead bird and a half-eaten frog into the tent and left them under my nose as a present. I don't know how it happened, but somehow *by accident* these dead things got into William and Mel's slippers while they were still sleeping!

I was downstairs having breakfast when my big sister woke up and put her toes in the frog. Her screams carried right through the floorboards. Me, Ralph and Aaron nearly choked on our cereal. But

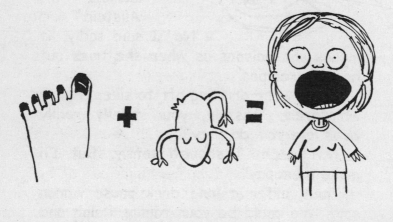

when Mel's screams woke up William and he squelched the bird and started screaming too, that was payback-tastic!

Five minutes later, Mum came downstairs carrying the squashed frog and bird in a dustpan.

'Alistair,' she said, 'did you have anything to do with this?'

'No, Mummy,' I said, innocently. 'I love my brother and sister. Besides, if I want to be a TV celebrity I have to be good, don't I? It must have been the cat!' Then while Mum went out to the dustbin, Aaron, Ralph and I burst out laughing! Unfortunately, I laughed so much I burped milk out of my nostrils and dribbled it into the marmalade. It was like having a nosebleed, only this blood was cold and had come out of a cow's udder. 'Mummy,' I cried when she came back in. 'I feel sick.' So Aaron and Ralph were sent home and I spent the day on the sofa wrapped in a warm blanket. Oh, poor, poor me! It did mean, however, that my big brother and sister weren't allowed to touch me!

Then Mum spoiled it all by bringing up the dreaded piano lesson with Mrs Muttley. I hate Mrs Muttley. She laughs like a hyena and shrieks so loud my eardrums bleed, but Mum's got it into her head that I'm going to be the next Charlotte Church. I have pointed out that Charlotte Church is a girl and signs, whereas I am a boy who plays the piano, but she's just thinking about the millions of pounds I could make her. In this respect, doing piano is just another form of child slavery that must be resisted. It doesn't matter that Mrs Muttley has breath like a camel and a neck like a turkey, Mum says I have to practise. But if I practise I'll get better and if I get better I'll have to have lessons for ever

and ever, and I think I'd rather eat warm horse manure!

'You've missed your last four piano lessons,' she said, 'because of too much home-work.' The old 'too much homework' excuse never fails! 'So I've rearranged your next lesson for three weeks on

Sunday. And you'll be pleased to hear I've managed to book it for two and a half hours to make up for all that lost time. Ten till twelve thirty. OK?' She watched my face fall. 'You're always free on Sundays.'

'But I'm thinking of starting to play Sunday rugby with Will.'

'You've never played rugby, Alistair. You hate sport, remember?' Her lips stiffened. 'You're doing piano.'

'But I've just thought,' I said. 'What if I suddenly become religious between now and three weeks on Sunday? And what if I have a long pray on the day? My fingers might be too tired to play the piano.' Mum was prepared to take the risk.

I hate Mum. I wish Aaron and Ralph *were* my family. We could be like

the Mafia and put Mrs Muttley in a concrete overcoat, then I wouldn't have to play that stupid, monotonous *March Of The One-Legged Elephant* ever again! Sadly though, in this backward country, children are still not allowed to divorce their parents. Maybe, instead of being brothers, Aaron, Ralph and me could have a secret club. We could call it the Revengers. Members could meet to discuss interesting and varied ways to zap my big brother and sister. Torture would be allowed. But *NO* mercy!

Have just made two secret phone calls. Aaron and Ralph also think that a secret club sounds wicked! They are massively up for it and have promised to bring evil thoughts into school tomorrow. I am so happy that I have just put a new sign on my bedroom door next to my picture of Gareth Southgate and my other three signs.

1) IF YOU KICK ME YOU ARE ONLY
KICKING YOURSELF!
(Zen and the art of surviving
big brothers and sisters)
2) NO MEMBER OF THE FURY
FAMILY MAY ENTER AT ANY TIME
UNLESS THEY SIGN A BIT OF PAPER
FREELY ADMITTING THAT
MASTER A. FURY ESQ. IS NOT ONLY
A TOTAL G, BUT A Q-T TOO!
3) KEEP OUT - TOXIC FARTS.

The new sign says,

BEWARE! JUDGEMENT DAY IS SOONER
THAN YOU THINK. THE COUNTDOWN
HAS BEGUN.

And I signed it

The Revengers.

I can't sleep I'm so excited.

I am keeping a daily score so that I can see all the time that I am the best!
Alistair 1 - Rest of Family 0

MONDAY

Not a good start to the day. Someone has drawn a bare bottom on my new sign in black felt tip and signed it WF. I suspect William.

Better news at breakfast. I was reading the back of the Coco Pops packet when suddenly I remembered the Spot The Ball competition that I had entered last month. This week they announce the result! And when I win I shall be famous, just like Charlotte Church, only (Mother, take note) *without* the piano.

Then things took a sharp turn for the worse again. Mum has started testing new recipes for her cookery show. I know I should say that she's the best cook in the world,* but the truth is even filthy flies won't eat her food.

*especially as I have to be nice to her to get on the telly

This is a list of some of her new recipes:

Fish eyes in goats cheese chowder
Polish vodka and raw beetroot soup

yvvurk

Bony fish pie with lentils
Snails tartare with sour cherry sauce
Maggoty pheasant and vinegar pie
Mashed black-eyed beancakes with
wildly wrinkled mushrooms

bleeurgh

Tooting green curry with lemongrass rice and extra large chilli-balls

vmmph

Broccoli soufflé with pears in marrowbone jelly.
Prune and carrot cake with aniseed marzipan
Liver and bacon ice-cream

She asked us what we thought. In my head I thought *PUKE!* but out loud I said, 'Delicious!' just to be nice. Nobody else said a word.

'Thank you, Alistair,' said my mum. 'It's nice to be appreciated. You can be my official taster.' I think I may have started something I'm going to regret.

A bit like flipping piano lessons

TOP SECRET!

First meeting of the Revengers in lunch break at school. Met in the Second Year loos where we would not be disturbed. Ralph stood at the door and kept all Second Years out. He was like a bouncer. It didn't matter how desperately boys wanted to go he just wouldn't let them in!

The Revengers have now got:

a) A secret handshake, which is so secret I've forgotten how it goes. Ralph wouldn't let us practise it in case someone was spying.

b) A secret password that a Revenger must say to another Revenger to identify himself. Anyone who doesn't know the secret password can't be a Revenger and anyone who isn't a Revenger can be killed. The secret password is 'Peanut butter and jam sandwiches'. Actually, it's more of a pass*phrase*.

c) A secret look. This look is a sort of scowl with a narrowing of the eyes. If any Revenger member sees another Revenger member doing this

Revenger look, the Revenger member knows that the Revenger member doing the Revenger look is in trouble, and the Revenger member not doing the Revenger look will immediately spring to the aid of the Revenger member doing the look. It's simple but brilliant too.

d) Invisible ink for writing invisible messages like this one:

I love Pamela Whitby. I love Pamela Whitby. I love Pamela Whitby. I love Pamela Whitby. I love Pamela Whitby. I love Pamela Whitby.

Nobody knows this secret. Not even Pamela Whitby. I think I'd die if anyone told her.

How quickly does this ink go invisible? I have waited one hour now and still no sign of vanishing.

2 hours – the writing's still there.

3 hours – I'm really worried that we have

Pamela Whitby must never ever ever see this diary!

31

been sold invisible ink that is not invisible.

We sorted out the club rules:

1. **No taking revenge out on another Revenger member.**
2. **No cowardly behaviour in the face of the enemy.**
3. **All sweets must be shared.**

Afterwards, we dreamed up the most worst revenges on my big brother for being so mean the night before and scaring our pants off with the wailing ghost thing. I thought of piranha fish in his bath. 'It'd be funny if I swapped the soap for a piranha fish,' I said. 'Imagine my  big brother singing in the bath. '*La la la la la! Oh I think I'll just soap my willy now.*' He takes the soap out of the soap dish and . . .

'*aaaaaaagh!*' Lots of blood. Lots of tears, and one big brother leaps out of bath minus dangly part of his anatomy! Ha ha!'

Ralph thought of cutting William's legs off just below the knee so that he'd be forced to see the world from down where we were. 'Then he might be more nicer to people who are shorter than him,' he said. But we thought leg-chopping was going a bit too far. Breaking his knees with a base-ball bat would have been all right, but actual severance, no.

But Aaron's idea was the best. He thought of cutting the brakes on William's bike, then telling him that there were naked women at the bottom of a really steep hill and that if he cycled really fast down the really steep hill he might just see them! Ha ha! Splat!

After our meeting, when we finally left the loos, we found hundreds of Second Years hopping and fidgeting outside. It was like a Martian had landed and given them all a disease of wet trousers. Teachers stood around looking confused and not knowing why everyone was damp.

Have just eaten Mum's supper and am lying in bed next to a bucket, with sheets of newspaper on my duvet in case I'm sick again. We had fish eyes in goats cheese chowder. That's blinking soup to those who've never had it! When Mum produced it Dad left the table. 'I'm not eating that,' he said.

'Neither am I,' said William. 'I'll have toast.'

'Me too,' said Mel.

'And me!' I added.

'But I thought you were going to be my little taster,' she said. 'I thought you were going to be nice to me, Alistair, so that you could come on the telly with me.'

I wanted to be nice, but when she pushed the bowl in front of me, the whites of the eyes

This is just another example of the chips of the world being stacked against me like a potato mountain.

TONS OF TONS ←WILL

rolled over in the soup and stared deep inside me, just like William always did before he used me as a punchbag.

'Shall I serve him?' sniggered William, stirring the pot.

If I was living in the future I'd have my neck changed for a spring. Then the next time William smacked me, my head would spring forward and nut him!

'Aren't *you* having any?' I said to Mum.

'No,' she replied. 'I don't like eyes.'

'BUT NEITHER DO I!' I wailed.

'Don't be so selfish,' said my big brother. 'If Mummy's gone to the trouble of cooking

it for you, you can *see* your way to eating it!' He was loving this.

'Besides,' added Mum. 'You don't know you don't like eyes until you've tried them.'

Well, now I *have* tried them, and surprise, surprise . . . I DON'T LIKE EYES!

Major planning under the bedclothes:

Aim
to get back into Mum's good books and pay back target.

Target
William, of course.

Reason
For encouraging Mum to make me eat food with eyelids.

Weapon

 Chocolax – *'the laxative that keeps you going and going and going and going . . .'*

Ha ha!

The eyes have it 2-2.
But looking forward to BIG score tomorrow!

TUESDAY

Before school I gave Mum a big kiss and said, 'Thank you for those delicious eyeballs last night, Mummy. You're such a good cook. Could we have banana splits tonight, do you think? With crumbly chocolate flakes on? Would that be OK, Mummy?'

She went all gooey-eyed and kissed me back. 'Who's a little charmer,' she said. And I turned away as if I was embarrassed, but I wasn't really. I was being dead cunning.

Brilliant acting

Before supper, while I just happened to be in the kitchen, somehow, *by accident*, the normal chocolate flakes got scraped off William's banana split and laxative chocolate got

37

grated on instead! When I have finished with William, he will be spending the whole night with smelly belly and it serves him right-up-his-popo!

I wanted Mum to cook something disgusting again for supper, so that William would refuse it and be really really hungry for his pudding. Then he would eat his banana split like a starving dog and not notice the funny-tasting chocolate! But what does Mum do? She only serves beef-burger and chips! It's not fair! Beefburger and chips is William's favourite – he always eats too much! By the time pudding came round he was stuffed.

'Go on,' I said, pushing my revenge across the table. 'Have a banana split.'

'Can't!' he said. 'Too full.'

'Yes you can!' I shouted. 'You have to!'

'If you want it, Alistair, just say so,' said my dad. 'I'm sure William won't mind.'

'I don't want it,' I said.

'Yes you do,' said Mum. 'You were the one who asked for banana splits this morning. Go on, Alistair, treat yourself.' How could I tell her it wasn't a treat?

'Alice,' said William smugly. 'You haven't done something naughty to my banana split, have you?'

'No,' I said, over-defensively.

'Then eat it,' he said. And I was stuffed.

In both senses of the word. ↑⌐

It is four o'clock in the morning. It feels like my guts have just been squeezed through a mangle. Never again. I have spent the last five hours on the loo with my bottom making noises like a hippopotamus sucking a thick milkshake.

William heard me groaning, came in and laughed, and said what a shame it was that I had a bad dose of banana splats. If I had not been at death's door I would have hit him on the head with a loo brush and locked him in the bathroom with the smell. As it was, I was sitting there for so long, I read six comics and a magazine called *Top Girl*, which had a quiz in it. **BIG SISTERS – HOW MUCH DO YOU REALLY HATE YOUR LITTLE BROTHER?** Mel had filled it in and scored loads and loads! – the highest score possible. I wish I knew more about electricity, because I'd really like her door handle to somehow get wired up to the mains *by accident* and give her a huge electric shock. But I only know about insects and stuff, so I took the torch into the garden and dug up some worms, which, *by accident*, somehow got lost in her socks.

Unexpected banana bummer 2-5

WEDNESDAY

Mum had to chuck a bucket of cold water over Mel this morning. She had hysterics when she put her socks on. Actually it was me who had hysterics, she just had a screaming fit. It was the funniest thing I'd ever seen! That was when the phone rang.

My prayers have been answered! I am really close to being famous and wearing dark glasses all the time! The woman on the phone said that I have reached the last six in the Coco Pops Spot The Ball FA Cup Challenge. If I win I will get a phone call in a week's time telling me how to collect my prize – three tickets to the FA Cup Final! I will take Aaron and Ralph. Between you and me, Diary, I only entered the competition to annoy William. I hate football, but he worships it, so if I win I shall go without him and really upset him. Seeing William seething with envy is definitely worth ninety boring minutes of my time!

When I got off the phone Mum asked me it I'd lost weight. She thought I looked thinner than last night. I told her I'd been banana-ed and did indeed feel a little drained. She told me to go back to bed, which was good in one way, but bad in two others, because Mum brought me a left-over bowl of goats cheese chowder with fish eyes in, and after her worm trauma, Mel was allowed to stay off school too.

She pushed notes under my bedroom door all day, calling me a poisonous little toad and threatening to get her Luke to break my legs. So I ran downstairs shouting, 'Mummy! Mel's calling me horrible names!'

And Mel charged in after me shouting, 'Well it's his fault! He knows I hate wriggly things. Tell him, Mummy. Tell him that if he does it again I'm allowed to kill him and you won't mind.' My mum was up to her elbows in stuffed prunes and said, 'Whatever, darling.' Which shows you in one sentence what a cruel and evil mother she can be.

I told my dad what Mel had said when he came home early before lunch. He's the boss at the local leisure centre. They'd just got a new television for the gym and he'd brought it home to try it out. He was lying on the sofa watching golf.

'Fetch us a beer, Alistair.'

'Is what you're doing really work?' I asked.

'Oh yes,' he said. 'Highly skilled. And some crisps.'

'Did you know that Mum said Mel could kill me today?' I told him.

To which my dad replied, 'Golf buggies are brilliant though, aren't they? If I played golf I wouldn't walk anywhere. I'd have a chauffeur to drive me.' What was the point?

If I disappeared off the face of the earth tomorrow would I be missed? Would my family weep and wail and tear their hair out? Or would they have a nice lunch and watch the golf?*

When William came home I was watching cartoons and sitting in the comfy armchair. He up-ended the chair, shook me out and turned over to women's football.

'But you don't like women's football,' I protested.

'No, but neither do you, and that's the most important thing,' he smirked.

'Dad!' I moaned. 'Dad! Dad! Dad!' But Dad was asleep, so somehow I slipped and *by accident* punched his leg. 'Dad, William's just thrown me out of the armchair. *And* he's just turned over and I was watching!'

'Fried egg, double bubble and beans,' said Dad. He was sleep-talking.

'Anyway,' I said to William, wheeling out my big gun. 'I'm probably going to the FA Cup Final with Ralph and Aaron.'

'What?' he gasped. 'How?'

'They're phoning me next week to tell me if I've won the tickets.'

'Oh, but that's not fair!' he whined. 'You know I love football more than you.'

'Really?' I said. 'If only I'd known.' I was making out like that was the first I'd ever heard of it.

'And I've *always* wanted to see the FA Cup Final,' he said. By now I was smirking. 'Why are you taking Aaron and Ralph instead of me? I'm your brother.'

'Because Aaron and Ralph are my friends,' I said. 'I like them!'

Then Mel came in to watch MTV, but there was a snake in a video so she screamed and ran upstairs to phone her boyfriend instead.

Supper was bony fish pie with lentils and I was sick. While I had my head down the loo, Mum started crying because none of her family liked her food. Her  sobs echoed up the pipes like a ghostly wail from another world. It crossed my mind that maybe I *was* dead. There was certainly nothing left inside me. I was like an Egyptian mummy – perfect on the outside but empty within.

Before I went to sleep, Dad came up to see me. He was wearing his cheesy face, like a holy vicar who has something deep and meaningful to say.

46

'Just wanted a word,' he said thought-fully. 'Your mother and I were hoping that your behaviour might improve, Alistair, if we promised you could appear on the telly. But it hasn't, has it? It's got worse.'

I wanted to explain that it wasn't my fault. That William and Mel were always the ones who started it. That I was only ever the victim. But I knew he wouldn't believe me. So instead, I said nothing and put on a face that looked like I was inter-ested in what he was saying. He sat down on the edge of the bed and I knew I was in for a serious man to man chat. Dad's chats are famous. He thinks we'll remember them for the rest of our lives and pass his wisdom on to our children, but I wouldn't be so cruel.

'Son,' he said, 'life is a bit like a game of tug and war.'

'Tug *of* war,' I said.

'That's what I said,' he said, 'tug and war
. . . in which he who pulls the hardest often
does not win. Whereas he who tugs just a
little bit at a time often edges it.'

'But that's not true,' I said. 'If I gave
one huge tug while you were giving little
tiny ones I'd pull you over.'

'It's a saying, Alistair. I'm not saying it's
always right. It's just something to think
about.'

'I shall learn it by heart,' I said.

'So can I tell your mum you're going to
keep her food down from now on?'

'I'll inform my stomach,' I said.

'Good. And practise your piano?'

'Just about to do some,' I lied sweetly.

Dad took a deep breath. 'It's just that
whenever there's trouble at home, Alistair,
you're always there.'

'That's because I
live there,' I said.

KNOW THIS PARENTS!

When I can swim and have conquered my fear of sharks, and can build a shelter, and fly a small plane, and eat coconuts and berries, and have bought myself a pair of flip flops to walk on hot sand,* I am moving to a desert island with only *one* phone and *not* giving my family the number!

Win some, lose some, sick some up 5-6

THURSDAY

Woke up in a bad mood. I think it's hunger. I haven't eaten proper food for two days. Went back to school with a note from Mum and immediately got into trouble. Miss Bird, my form teacher, wanted to know why I hadn't done my History homework – collecting information about my ancestors for a family tree.

'I've been ill,' I said. 'I had food poisoning.'

'That's a lie,' she said. 'Your mother's note says you've been "under the weather". "Under the weather" is no excuse for not doing your homework, Fury. You have till Wednesday or it's a detention!' This was a bad day getting worse! I hated Mum for not owning up to being a poisoner and I hated Miss Bird for always giving me detentions and lines and extra work for no reason.

STOP THIS TORTURE

This is Miss Bird:

We call her Pigeon because she's got a beaky nose and waddles when she walks like she's got a fifty-pence piece clenched between her buttocks.

Pamela Whitby says Miss Bird takes it out on me, because she teaches cooking and hates my mum for making money out of

rubbish recipes that she could cook with her eyes closed. But when you think about it, if Miss Bird cooks with her eyes closed, that's exactly why my mum's a famous cook and Miss Bird will never be anything but a scummy teacher with a squint. One day I'll tell her that.

Was very polite to Mum when I got home. With my TV celebrity status at stake, I did not want to upset her again. 'Just off to practise my piano,' I said. Then, 'Oh by the way, why did you not write "food poisoning" in my note?'

'Because I did not poison you,' she said.

'I think you did,' I said. 'Twice.'

'Not deliberately.' Mum was blushing. 'Besides, before I put

my recipes in a book, I've got to make sure they're fit for human consumption.'

Gasp! Horror! It's a sad day when you discover that your own mother is using you as a guinea pig! 'Aren't I human too?' I cried, choking back bitter tears of rejection. 'If the food's *not* fit to eat you'll kill me first!'

'You're not human,' interrupted Mel. 'You're an evil swamp monster with the mind of a lavatory bowl!' That does it! The gloves are off. Nobody calls me a swamp monster and lives to tell the whole family again and again at every Sunday lunch from now till Christmas. Mel deserves everything the Revengers can throw at her!

And I'm not practising Mrs Muttley's stupid piano either!

WANTED

For crimes against A. Fury, the beauty industry and the human race.
THE REVENGERS

Napoleon has done a bunk. Nobody's seen him for a couple of days and Mel blames me. I know she doesn't care really. She hates that cat, but loves any chance of getting me into trouble. Only now it's not just me, is it? Because now I have the power that comes from being a Revenger!

Had the second secret meeting of the Revengers at break, and, based on the phobia of the target, came up with an absolutely brilliant evil secret revenge plan.

14 pairs of wet trousers this time!

54

Obviously, I can't tell you who the target of this brilliant evil secret revenge plan is in case my big sister reads this diary, but I *can* say that it's payback for everything bad she's ever done or said to me, and rats are only *part* of the surprise! It's going to be brilliant and secret. And evil of course.

Actually between you and me, Diary, I'm rather nervous. Accidentally torturing Mel with a snake was Ralph's idea after I'd made the mistake of saying that she didn't like them. But I don't think I want a snake. They're cold and dangerous, especially if they wriggle up your trousers. And if they get into your bedroom, they use your face as a pillow apparently. But Ralph told me it was the only way to give Mel what was coming to her and Aaron agreed. So I lost.

Napoleon is still at large. Mum says that if he's not back by tomorrow we're going to have to start a search with tree posters and everything. Dad says we should search the Island of Elba because Napoleon will probably be there, but I don't know where that is and anyway I don't plan to do any searching at all. He's not *my* hot-water bottle.

A good Revenge never forgets!

I placed an anonymous advert in *Loot*:

WANTED –
GLASS TANK
AND RAT CAGE –
CONTACT
THE REVENGERS

and paid for it with Dad's credit card. When the lady on the other end of the phone asked me if I was old enough to have a credit card, I told her I was forty-four.

'I only sound like I'm eleven, because I'm the product of a horrible scientific experiment. Years ago, they tried to make a human fly by stitching the wings of a bat onto a boy. That was me. I've still got the wings, but now I've got a squeaky voice too.'

'Is the cage for you?' asked the lady.

'Can't answer that now,' I said, 'I really must hang upside down from the ceiling. Bye.'

I needed at least £30 to buy the tank and cage, and the snake as well, and the food too, because snakes love live rats apparently. Make that £60.

Asked parents what they'd most like to see me do with my life. Dad said play for England. Mum said play piano at the Albert Hall. I said I'd do both if they paid me to practise, but they refused. So I asked for jobs around the house. Suggested that bed making and room tidying were worth at least £5 each per day.

'I'm not paying you to make your own bed,' said Dad. 'You should be doing that anyway.'

'Like brushing your teeth,' said Mum.

'All right,' I said. 'How about I refuse to

brush my teeth unless you give me money?'

↑ Never seen a mouth

'That's blackmail,' he said.

'Yes,' I said. 'What's wrong with that?' I also had another brilliant idea, that they could pay me for *not* picking my nose and *not* leaving my flies undone! They said they'd see what they could find for me to do, but only if I told them what I wanted the money for.

'A pet,' I said.

'You've got Mr E and Napoleon,' they said.

'A normal pet,' I said.

'Like what?'

'A crocodile!' I said.

'No!' they screamed.

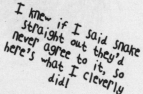

I knew if I said snake straight out they'd never agree to it, so here's what I cleverly did!

'OK, a vulture,' I said.
'**No!**' they yelled.

'How about a snake then?'
'Oh all right, but only a little one?'

Size doesn't matter where Mel's concerned! Me 8– Them 6

SATURDAY

Dad said he was thinking of building an extension to the kitchen and was I interested in doing the work?

'Will I have to climb a ladder?' I asked. Dad said I would, so I said I'd do it, because climbing ladders is fun. 'But I'll need a book, or something, to copy,' I said. 'I've never built an extension before.'

'Haven't you?' laughed Dad. 'You'll pick it up.'

'And how much will you pay me?' I asked.

'Six thousand pounds,' he said, 'but I want it done by lunchtime.' And he walked away. I stood there all morning waiting for

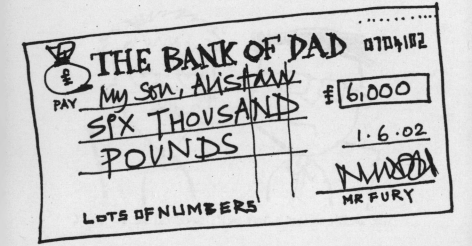

THE BANK OF DAD · 0704182

PAY My son, Alistair · £ 6,000

SIX THOUSAND POUNDS

1.6.02

MR FURY

LOTS OF NUMBERS

him to come back, but he never did. Sadly I don't know what an extension looks like or I could have made a start – or maybe even finished it, which would have been good. As it is, I am now £6,000 short.

No lunch today, because big sisters and parents were having a huge row over Luke. He's asked her to a weekend party in the middle of her exams, and Mel's said yes without asking Mum and Dad.

'I'm sixteen!' she yelled. 'I'm old enough to marry him. You can't stop me!'

'I thought it was just a party,' said Dad. 'Where did the dreaded "M" word spring from?'

'You're not going,' said Mum. '*After* your exams, that's fine, but not *during*!'

'But I love him!' wailed Mel.

'Good, then he won't mind waiting a few days,' said Mum.

'That's not fair!' screamed my big sister, kicking a chair across the floor. 'It's *my* life!' Then she stormed out, shouting, 'I wish I was dead and living somewhere else!'

And when I cheered and said, 'Great! Can I have your room when you go?' she turned round and slapped me so hard across the

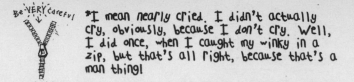

*I mean *nearly* cried. I didn't actually cry, obviously, because I *don't* cry. Well, I did once, when I caught my winky in a zip, but that's all right, because that's a man thing!

---

ear that I heard bells and wind, like I was sitting with goats on the side of a mountain.

And when I cried,* Mum said, 'Serves you right, you little troublemaker!' Huh! And there was innocent-little-me thinking it was Mel who was causing all the trouble!

Sometimes I think, in the history of mankind, that there has only ever been one person who was worse off than me, apart from the Elephant Man obviously, and

Gareth Southgate when he missed that penalty,* and that is the Queen's horse for having her big bottom sitting on him all the time, and Chips from the *Dandy*.

* Sorry. That's two.

The 'clip-round-the-ear-from-Mel' incident has had two effects. 1) She's really asked for it this time. 2) It has brought my frail mind under control. I no longer fear snakes. Bring on the Boa of Revenge!

Today, I am the slapped, but tomorrow I will be the slapper! 8-8

Hoovered the stairs = 50p.

Washed the bath = 20p.

Walked the dog = 75p.

Made posters for Lost
Cat = 1p each.

It is not enough. Revenge,
however sweet, does not
come cheap.

Granny Constance came to lunch. She was impressed with the way I cleared the table and did the washing up, but was shocked to find out that I was only doing it for hard cash. I took her for a walk in the park and showed her the ducks.

'They're extra,' I said.

'Whatever do you mean?' she asked.

'Nothing,' I smiled. But when I got home I charged Mum £1.50 for the walk and added on a surcharge of 25p for 'brightening

Granny's day with pond life'. Then I washed the car, polished the silver, weeded the front path, unloaded the dishwasher, wiped the finger-plates, picked up rubbish and combed the cat and dog with Mum's hair-brush.

It is the end of the working day and I have earned a mighty £11.35, but at what cost to my health? I am exhausted. I am more wrung out than a flannel. In the name of revenge, I have slaved for nearly two WHOLE HOURS today! But remember, I am *more* tired than a slave would be, because I haven't stopped for tea and biscuits or anything!

'Piano practise?' asked Mum.

'Too tired!'

Dad just came in and asked if I was still trying to earn money to buy a tank and a rat cage. I told him I was. 'Like the ones we've got in the attic?' he asked. I could not believe it! He'd had them in the attic all along. All that work for nothing!

'You might have said!' I said.

'Yes, but if I had,' he smiled, 'you wouldn't have done all those chores for me, would you?'

I feel used. Own goal 8-9

64

I don't even know who's playing in the FA Cup Final, and quite frankly I don't give a monkey's. Winning the tickets and *not* giving one to William is all I care about! He's tried to be nice to me twice now, but he's *not* coming!

Must keep this secret from Dad. If he finds out he's bound to take William's side and make me give him a ticket. Sometimes I wonder if Dad is my real dad at all – after all, he loves sport and I don't. And he always wants me to change who I am, as if who I am isn't good enough. Maybe I'm different, because I *am* different. Sets you thinking.*

After school, Ralph, Aaron and I went to the pet shop and bought a boa constrictor called Alfred. He cost £12, which was cheaper than I was expecting, but snakes are sold by the metre and Alfred is only twenty-two centimetres long. The man in the shop says he'll grow to three metres. When he asked if

*Sometimes I am awash with maturity

I wanted any food, I said I didn't have enough money and would have to come back for some rats when I did. So the nice man gave me two frozen mice to keep the wolf from Alfred's door.

I cycled home with Alfred in my ruck-sack and slipped him into one of William's rugby socks. Then I tied up the top so he couldn't get out, tiptoed into my big sister's room and put the sock under her duvet with a note attached: MY NAME IS REVENGE.

At supper I could hardly contain myself. I was so full of nervous anticipation that I ate two helpings of snails tartare thinking it was pasta. My mum called me her little angel and I let her give me a big hug. It was the perfect moment to ask the question I'd been dying to ask for weeks. 'Have you spoken to Michael yet?' I asked, 'about me being on the telly?' Michael was Mum's TV producer.

'I will,' she said. 'I definitely heard her say, 'I will.'

Went to bed early and lay in the dark waiting for big sister to come upstairs. I heard her feet climbing. Then I heard shuffling, followed by rustling, screaming, crying, running, stamping, howling, sobbing, thumping and more screaming!

I ran onto the landing where Mel was dancing naked round an empty sock. She was throwing her clothes off, shouting, 'Is it on me? Is it on me?'

By now Mum and Dad were up the stairs

and William was trying to take photos of Mel to sell to his mates at school, and I was standing there like a little angel, going, 'What is the matter, Mel? Have you seen a ghost?' But under my breath I was snickering, because I knew what I'd done!

'Who put the snake in Melanie's bed?' That was Mum. She sounded stressed.

'Was it you, Alistair?'

'No,' I said. But then I remembered that I'd told them I wanted to buy one so I changed my tune. 'I mean, yes, Mummy. I thought Mel liked snakes. I was sharing my new pet with her. Was that not a nice thing to do?'

'You know snakes make my flesh crawl!' shuddered Mel.

'No, I didn't know that,' I said sweetly. 'It's only a *little* baby boa constrictor. It's lovely really. Would you like to see it eat a mouse?' Mel screamed again. 'Oh, that reminds me. Has anyone found Napoleon, because this snake could easily gobble him up by accident!'

mmphmeowmph

'Stop it, Alistair!' shouted Mum. But Henry VIII didn't stop chopping off his wives' heads just because his mum told him

69

to. It was too much fun.

'Don't be such a girl,' I grinned. 'It's not nasty. It's natural. Besides, you can hardly hear the crack of the mouse's skull as it's crushed by the snake's jaws. And you won't see much blood at all. Unless the snake's sick, of course. Then you'll see everything – heart, liver, lungs, brain . . .'

I was sent to my room.

23.25 – It's 2 hours later and I still feel brilliant!

Result! 100-9

Woke remembering poxy History home-work, but refuse to let it spoil last night's brilliant victory. I shall ask Mum and Dad about their ancestors tonight.

Outside the bathroom I had the power over Melanie, who couldn't look me in the eye. She was still upset, because now she thought my snake had eaten her cat! She was crying when she told me to help look for Napoleon.

'Go on,' said Mum. 'Do something useful for once, Alistair.'

'I can't,' I said. 'I've got to practise my piano.' Then to my mother's astonishment I went back into my bedroom and ran my finger up the keyboard, but half the keys were sticking and when I thumped middle C there was a loud squelch.

I have one tiny problem. Now that revenge is done and the joke is over, I am left with a snake. As I explained to Ralph at the second secret meeting, I don't like snakes and haven't the foggiest how to look after them. Do I have to clean out the tank? Do I have to scoop up its poop in a plastic bag? I don't even know if it does poop. It could be pellets or guacamole, like iguanas do. And how do I feed it? Do I just drop the frozen mice into the cage and let the snake do the rest, or do I have to cut the mice up and cook them with onions and salad and dollops of tomato ketchup? And what about exercise? Do I put the snake on a lead and take it for a walk with Mr E? Too many questions and not enough answers.

Because he is not the most popular guest we've ever had in our house, I shall take Alfred to school today and hope he likes noise and lots of people.

No idea

I hid him in my rucksack and sat him on the draining board all through breakfast without anyone knowing! Not even Mum's producer, Michael, knew when he arrived for a meeting. He sat down right in front of Alfred and didn't have a clue he was there, and Michael's supposed to be in TV where everyone is always looking out for funny pets to put on programmes. So he can't be very good at his job.

Apparently, Mum's first programme is going out in ten days time and the BBC are worried because they haven't seen what's in it yet. Mum's bottom lip trembled as she told Michael that she had been trying to get her recipes together, but she'd had problems.

'Really?' I said. 'What are they?' I didn't realize parents had problems. I thought all problems stopped when your big brother and sister left home. She meant *me*. 'I beg your pardon?' I said. '*I'm* the problem?' And when I casually asked Mum if Michael knew that I was going to be her helper this series, she told me to shut up.

'Celia darling, the bottom line is this,' said Michael. 'We *must* record the programme by Friday week or we won't hit transmission. And no transmission means no series.'

Mum nodded. 'Michael,' she said, 'my recipes will be ready even if it kills me.'

'Or *me*,' I said jokingly, but nobody laughed.

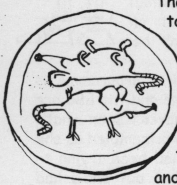

That was when Michael took a great big sniff and asked Mum what was cooking that smelled so delicious. She said she didn't know.

'Mice,' I said. 'I decided to cook them.' The microwave pinged and I took out two piping hot pink mice on a plate.

'Tell me they're marzipan!' squeaked Michael.

'No, they're mice,' I said.

'And you eat them?'

'Eat them!' I said. 'What do you think I am? They're for my snake.'

I could not have had any idea what was going to happen next.

Alfred smelled the mice and wriggled out the top of my rucksack. Then thinking Michael's blond hair was a delicious guinea pig the boa constrictor wrapped its coils around his head. Michael screamed and sprang up from the table, but this just made Alfred squeeze harder, and the harder Alfred squeezed the higher Michael's hair rose off his scalp revealing a bald head underneath. Then suddenly the hair pinged off like an elastic band and flopped into a saucepan. 'Oh it's a wig!' I cried. And with that comment I lost all chance of Mum asking Michael to make me a TV star. I knew

that, because ten seconds later she threw me and the snake out of the house.

At school, the snake caused even more chaos. I was only showing Ralph and Aaron how its constricting coils could fire globs of toothpaste out of a tube when the girls came in from the playground. They shrieked, tucked their skirts into their knickers and jumped on top of their desks. It has to be said, Pamela Whitby looked easily the most gorgeous, until she fainted and knocked a tooth out.

Panos Papayoti, who's huge and incredibly hairy for eleven, and knows all sorts of rude stuff that none of us understands, winked and said, "If you think that tucking your skirts into your knickers is going to save you from the snake, girls, think again!" Nobody knew what he was talking about.

Then Pigeon came in and a glob of toothpaste hit her right on the tip of her beak. She flapped her wings and dragged me to the front. "What is the meaning of this?" she squawked, slapping Alfred on the head. "And don't tell me it's a snake, because I hate snakes".

"Oh it's not a snake", I lied. "It's a legless, long-tailed lizard!"

'It is a snake!'

cried the girls, at which Pigeon hopped on top of the desks to join them.

'Alistair Fury!'

she shouted.*
'Have five gold stars for bringing in your pet and now take it home!'
'What?' I was confused. Pigeon was being nice. 'But I'm not allowed to leave till the end of school, miss,' I said.

'Take ten gold stars!'

she shrieked.
'Don't you want to stroke it?'

'No!'

she said

'Make it fifteen!'

'Or watch it dislocate its jaw?'

✦

'How many gold ✦ stars do you want to remove that revolting reptile from my classroom?'

That was when I realized she was scared.

'Twenty,' I said. I never got gold stars and twenty was more than most people got in a term.

My joy at being the best-behaved boy in the class meant that I went home feeling ten metres tall. All I wanted was to show off my gold stars to my family and use them to bribe my way back onto Mum's TV show, but when I rushed into the hall, my big brother and sister slammed the sitting-room door in my face, and my own mother made it perfectly clear that I was less important to her than a snail soufflé.

'Go away, Alexander. I'm trying to cook!'

My name is Alistair! Not Alexander. Not Alice. ALISTAIR.

A for 'Ard-done-by
L for last
I for Ignored
S for Sweet-as-sugar-pie
T for Terminator

A for Animal handler
I for Innocent
R for **REVENGE**

Nobody is talking to me. I have been cast out into the wilderness and it's all Alfred's fault!

'This is the last time any of your family will speak to you,' said Mel, pinning my shoulder to the wall, 'until you apologize for being so heartless and cruel to me, and promise that your snake will never – that's NEVER – leave your room, unless of course it's dead.' Then she added. 'And it looks like *I'm* helping Mum on the telly now, because you can't behave.'

What had seemed like a brilliant idea yesterday, now seemed triple pants!

Not only that but to do my History homework I have to talk to Mum and Dad about their ancestors. But I can't talk to them if they won't talk to me. I'm going to get a detention and that's Alfred's fault too!

Later, when the phone rang, William

answered it and said, 'Alistair? No I'm afraid he's not in. Bye.'

It was too much. I burst out of my bedroom. 'Who was it?' I yelled. 'Was it the Coco Pops Challenge? Have I won?' But William said nothing. I banged on his bedroom door. 'William,' I screamed, 'you have to tell me. Who was it?'

My dad came out of the sitting room. 'What's going on, Alistair?' he said.

'Ssssssh!' hissed Mel, clamping her hand over Dad's mouth. 'No talking! He's been sent to Coventry. Now go back inside and

forget you've got a younger son!' Then she pushed him through the door and stuck her tongue out at me.

And even later still, I heard footsteps pad across my bedroom floor. As I rolled over in bed a hand slipped over my mouth.

'Weurreugh?' I said.

It was Mum and Dad looking nervous. 'William and Mel must never know that we've been in here tonight?' hissed Dad. 'This conversation never happened,' added Mum, checking over her shoulder. 'We're still not talkling to you Alistair. Understood?' Dad wiped his lips and stared me in the eye. 'We're just here to say, get rid of that snake or...' He stopped.

'Or nothing', said Mum, looking crossly at him. 'Just get rid of that snake. And don't ask us to do it, because we're too scared, all right!'

It is eleven o'clock. I can't sleep. I can hear William singing to himself next door. 'I'm going to see the cup! I'm going to see the cup! E-I-addio, I've got three tickets to see the cup!' What does he mean?

WEDNESDAY

At breakfast, I begged my big brother to tell me if I'd won the tickets, but he wouldn't talk. He just smiled and sealed his lips with an imaginary zip.

'You're lying,' I said. 'You're winding me up. I can tell.' But I couldn't really. I didn't have a clue what the truth was. I can't take much more of this silence! It is torture. If it goes on any longer I shall have to call the RSPCA and report my family for child cruelty.

It struck me on the way to school that maybe the school might like to have Alfred as an interesting specimen for the Biology labs, but when I mentioned it to Pigeon, she threw a blackboard rubber at my head, burst into tears and erupted in huge white goosebumps. She didn't look like a pigeon any more. She looked like a turkey.

'Shall I take that as a no then?' I said. As she tried to say yes a bubble of snot blew up out of her nose like bubblegum.

When Pigeon had composed herself with sweet tea, she chose me out of the whole class to stand up and talk about my family's ancestors.

Why does that always happen? If I've

done the homework I'm *never* asked! I don't know anything about my family except that somewhere down the line I must have been related to the Invisible Man, which explains why nobody ever notices me! So I made something up instead.

'My family is all descended from apes,' I said. 'Except Melanie and William who *are* apes!' Sometimes I think I'm a genius. Pigeon didn't think so though. I got that detention. Thank you, Alfred.

After detention, I took the snake back to the pet shop and tried to give him back. 'It's damaged goods,' I said. 'It's faulty. It's not like a normal pet, it keeps upsetting people.' But that was not the shopkeeper's problem apparently. He opened the door to the street. 'If it was a toaster you'd replace it,' I said as he patted me on the head and ushered me out. 'It's past its sell-by date!' The door shut and Alfred and I found ourselves out on the pavement.

I hate this stupid scoring thing. It's meant to show that I'm brilliant, but how can it with this stupid snake that won't go away? Me 100- Them 99 still ahead by a rat's whisker, but only just!

More silence. No breakfast. Mel and William deliberately finished all the bread, milk and cereal before I came down. When I looked in the fridge it was full of Mum's TV food.

'What's this?' I asked Dad, picking up a green ring doughnut. 'Can I eat it?'

'It's toad in the hole,' he said. 'I wouldn't.'

'Shut up!' shouted Mel. 'Dad, you're useless. How will snake-boy ever learn his lesson if you keep talking to him?'

I definitely wish I'd never bought Alfred now. He was fun for ten minutes, but since then he's made my life a misery. If I ever want to hear the sound of a kindly human voice again that snake has got to go. But how?

And William won't stop smirking.

'We'll help you get rid of him,' said Ralph. 'Permanently.'

'You mean bump William off for good?' I said. 'It's not allowed, is it?'

'Not William, Alfred,' said Ralph. 'Wrap him up in brown paper and string, and post him to the Outer Hebrides.'

'He won't fit through the slot in the post box,' I said.

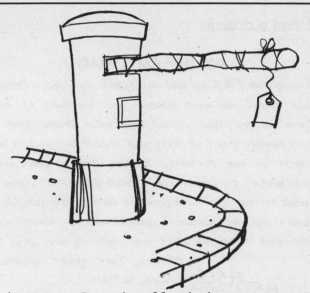

'Anyway, I can't afford the postage. I can't even afford to feed him.'

'Then *don't* feed him,' said Aaron. 'And when he dies and goes stiff, you can use him as a snooker cue!' I told them I felt like a murderer just talking about it, but they said that some murders were OK if nobody found out. I agreed to meet after school tomorrow to eliminate 'The Problem'.*

'But bring a sock,' I said.

'Why?' asked Aaron.

'As a hood. If I have to look at his innocent little eyes I won't be able to bash his brains out, will I!' Tomorrow it will all be over and I can get back to winning ways. 101-100

FRIDAY

I had a dream.

MY DREAM I HAD

I won the FA Cup last night, but the whole crowd was silent, because nobody was speaking to me. Even my dad, who should have been proud that I was playing sport at last, just stood there with his hands in his pockets, looking the other way, pretending to count the floodlights. And when I went to get the cup from the Queen she wouldn't give it to me, because I was wicked to animals, and she gave it to the next man instead, who was, of course, that great sporting hero, William.

The Revengers met secretly in my bedroom. I put a sign on the door to keep my family out:

BRING A
SNAKE
PARTY
EVERYONE WELCOME

We were not disturbed.

I put the sock over Alfred's head and bent a cotton bud into a U shape to make him a pair of ear-muffs. This stopped  him from freaking out while we ran through all the ways of murdering a snake we could think of. Shooting, stabbing, knotting, wringing, stretching, skinning, cooking, grating, chopping, slicing . . . it got quite gruesome, actually. Ralph suggested we did something where we didn't need to be there, like burying Alfred in the garden and blowing him up with dynamite, but I put my foot down.

'If we damage Mum's flowers she'll kill us!' I said.

In the end we just dumped him in the dustbin and put a brick on the lid to stop him climbing out.

BIG NEWS!

I have just discovered my conscience. I did not realize I had one. I am trying to get to sleep, but my conscience keeps waking me up. It won't let me forget the pathetic look on Alfred's face as I shut the dustbin lid. I wonder if Hell is as hot as everyone says it is? I shall buy sandals just in case.

Murderers are not worthy of points. 101-100

SATURDAY

Saved! Woke this morning and my conscience has gone again! I don't feel even slightly guilty about Alfred any more. In fact I've already forgotten what he looked like, which means I can't have loved him that much. The dastardly deed is done. I am free once again!

I rushed downstairs anxious to share my glorious news. I found Dad ironing his underpants in the kitchen.

'Dad!' I cried. 'I've done what everyone wanted! You can speak to me again!' But he was having trouble with his creases and growled at me. So I told Mel and William instead.

'He's just saying he's got rid of the snake to make us like him,' my big sister said to my big brother, making sure I could hear even though she wasn't talking to me. 'Well it won't work.'

'Mum!' I shouted, rushing into the dining room where she and Michael were tasting witchetty grubs au gratin. He was wearing a pink baseball cap in case the snake fell in love with his wig again. 'Mum! You can speak to me again, I've binned the sn—'

'OUT!'

Something has snapped in my head. I am how officially bored of being ignored. I've tried to be good. I've disposed of the snake. I've changed! But nothing's ever good enough for my family. If I was an orphan I'd get more love and attention, but I'm not, I'm just a poor, wronged child who needs nurturing! Well, if they want war, they can have war! I *will* be noticed again.

To do this, I need to make myself the centre of attention. Here's a list of ways I could do it.

1) Pack a bag and leave home, after turning off the fridge while it's full of Mum's food.

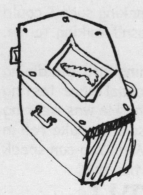

2) Build a cat-sized coffin containing all of Napoleon's favourite things – a tin of cat food, a ball with a bell in it, a dead mouse and a picture of his tail – and give it to Mel with my love.

3) Paint a message on a sheet – HELP ME. MY PARENTS ARE ALIENS. THEY ARE GOING TO EAT ME! – and hang it out of the window.

4) Pee in my big sister's bath.

5) Hide under my bed for a week and send hostage notes to my parents, saying things like, 'Pay up now or the boy loses a whole leg!' Mind you, if I was hiding under my bed, how would I get out to post the hostage notes? And what if they didn't pay and I really did have to cut off my own leg? Bad idea.

6) Alfred. Of course! Snakes alive! And the brilliance of this plan is I don't need to get Alfred back to do it!

I ran downstairs and burst into the dining room.

'Help!' I shouted. 'Help, the snake's escaped!' Michael leapt onto the table and screamed. Mum joined him. My big brother and sister rushed down from upstairs and my dad zipped in from the kitchen.

'What do you mean?' they shouted. 'You said you'd already got rid of the snake.'

'Lies!' I cried. 'All lies! I was covering up

for the fact that this morning the snake had grown! It was huge, far too big for the tank. I had to put my wardrobe on top of the lid to keep it in, but it must have muscled its way out – it's bigger than the Loch Ness Monster, honest it is – and slithered between the floorboards, because I can't find it. And it hasn't eaten for days so it's probably really really hungry. It could probably even eat a human! It could! And it's gone! Help! Everyone run!'

It worked.

Michael drove off so fast that his wig blew out the sunroof. Dad scooted off to his mum's where he said he'd left his glasses by mistake. My big, brave, hard-as-nails brother tried to be cool. He hung around long enough to give me a dead leg, but after that he bolted out the house saying he'd just remembered a twenty-four hour rave he had to go to. Mum ran to a wine bar, and Mel – big, sulky, I'm-the-

most-desirable-thing-on-the-planet Mel –
leapt upstairs wailing. 'That's it! I'm leaving
this slimy reptile-house. I'm going to live
with my boyfriend. Don't try to stop me!'
Nobody was trying to do anything, because
nobody was there. Then she phoned her
boyfriend and told him she was moving in
with him and his parents.

Luke the Puke

While they were on the
phone being sweethearts I
picked up the extension and
made a fart noise down the
receiver. Then I put on a high voice and
pretended to be my big sister. 'Oooh, sorry,

boyfriend Lukey darling, but I've got terrible farts since I had them beans for breakfast!' I was still laughing when Mel stormed down the stairs with a suitcase, pulled my hair and slammed out the front door. It was only when I stopped laughing that I realized my plan had been a miserable failure. How could I be the centre of attention when I was the only one in the house?

The Revengers came round. We ate something greasy with mushrooms from the fridge and discussed my problem.

'You do realize Alfred has to be found now, don't you?' said Ralph.

'Why?' I said.

'Because if your family thinks there's an uncaptured snake in the house they'll send you to Coventry for the rest of your life.' That meant we had to get him out of the dustbin and hide him somewhere where they'd find him!

Alfred looked well cross when we lifted the lid and picked him out of the dustbin with Dad's barbecue tongs.

'He could kill us,' said Aaron. 'And there's not a court in the land would convict him after what we've put him through.'

It was quite frightening hearing Alfred hiss and watching him twist his tail, but we got him into the kitchen and dropped him into a mixing bowl. Then we rolled him in pastry, lightly dusted him with flour and popped him into the fridge next to the other rolls of pastry that Mum had prepared for her television programme.

'We've got to think,' I said. 'Why would

he crawl into the fridge?' I needed a good answer in case I was asked.

'To hibernate,' said Aaron. 'They've got cold blood.'

'So why did he roll himself in pastry first?'

'Camouflage,' said Ralph. 'To hide amongst the pies!' So that was that. I'd covered my tracks. The snake had escaped and I '*did not know where it was*'!

Although I did obviously!

SUNDAY

Everyone came home eventually last night, except my big sister. I've said sorry so many times I've forgotten the meaning of the word, but it seems to have done the trick. I don't think I'm in Coventry any more. I think I'm back in Tooting.

Trouble with that was this:

'Alistair.' This is the first thing my mum said to me after my punishment was over. 'There's only one week to go before your two-and-a-half-hour piano lesson with Mrs Muttley, and I haven't heard you practise once.'

'Oh, but I have,' I said. 'I practise all the time when you're out of the house, and sometimes when you're in. But the pieces I'm playing are ever so soft – so soft that sometimes even I can't hear them myself. You've heard of pianissimo, well these pieces are silencissimo. It's very very hard.'

Mum was rolling out her cheese pastry when the snake flopped out. She made a strange high-pitched noise like a New York police siren. By the time I reached the kitchen, Dad was picking her up off the floor and she was gasping for air.

'Alfred was in my anchovy toasties!' she whispered. 'I was just going to chop up my pastry when it wriggled.' Now of course I had to pretend I was glad that Alfred had been found.

'So Alfred's still alive,' I cheered. 'Hooray!' I grabbed a saucepan and filled it with lukewarm water from the tap.

'If Mum has a heart attack you're to blame,' hissed my big brother. 'You're such a fool, Alice. If I was your father I'd put you across my knee and beat you with my slipper.'

'If you were my father I'd have a brain the size of an ant's kneecap!' I said, turning off the tap. 'I'm thawing the snake out.' Then I broke open Mum's pastry and popped a rather cold and stiff Alfred into his warm bath.

'Snakes can't swim,' said William.

'Can't they?' I said. Well Alfred couldn't. He'd sunk to the bottom of the pan. I

grabbed him out and rigged up a hammock with a J-cloth and two elastic bands, then stuck him back in the sling so that his body was underwater but his head was out. The colour flooded back into his cheeks.

That was when my big sister reappeared. Apparently, she'd spent a horrible night at her boyfriend's house. He'd made her sleep on the floor in case the beans made her fart.

'What beans?' said mum. 'You didn't eat beans. You hardly eat anything!'

'The beans that *he* made up on the telephone!' shouted Mel, pointing at me. I thought she was going to attack me, but I was wrong. Instead, she lunged forward, grabbed the pan with Alfred in, plonked it on the cooker and turned the heat up full.

'What are you doing?' I squealed.

'Boiled snake,' she said, leaving the room. 'I hate all of you!'

Poor Alfred. In the dustbin, out of the dustbin, in the fridge, out of the fridge, freezing cold one minute, boiling hot the next. It's a wonder he didn't bite anyone. He must be the best-tempered boa constrictor in the world. Either that or the best-cooked.

'First thing in the morning,' growled Dad, 'that snake goes!'

Early bath for me and snake
Me 150 - Them 125

103

Have not slept a wink. Alfred has been making funny gurgling noises all night. When I got up to check on him he was lying perfectly still with his eyes open and a lopsided grin on his face. He looks exactly like Jack Nicholson. I went into Mum and Dad's bedroom and told them Alfred was sick.

'It's three o'clock in the morning,' groaned my dad. 'Go away!'

'But he's ill,' I said. 'I can't chuck him away while he's ill. I might kill him.'

'We'll get rid of him when he's better,' mumbled my mum. 'Go back to bed.'

So now I'm back in bed, but I still can't sleep. Alfred's staring eyes are inside my head. I think he's gone mad. I think he's planning his revenge on me for putting him in the fridge! Why does everything go wrong in my life? How do you tell a snake you're sorry? And why aren't my friends here when I need them?

Friends. That's it! That's what's wrong. Alfred needs friends, a bit of company, someone to talk to. If I buy him some friends he'll like me again and stop wanting to kill me. There is only one problem. Animal friends cost money and I'm broke. I know a man who isn't though.

Unfortunately it was only four thirty in the morning and Dad was still asleep. So I made him a cup of coffee which somehow got spilled *by accident* over his sheets and woke him up. He leapt out of bed like a rocket. 'Dad,' I said, smiling. 'A week ago, I got twenty gold stars . . .'

'Aaaagh! My legs!' he cried. 'Call an ambulance!'

When I got back from

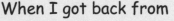

school, Dad was much better. He could walk without screaming. I asked him if he'd give me £30 for getting those gold stars. I was expecting applause. I was expecting whoops of joy and phone calls to relatives telling them how brainy I was. Instead I got this:

'What are gold stars?'

'They're what we get given at school for being good,' I said.

'For being good,' laughed Dad. 'I'm not giving you money for being good, Alistair. You should be good at all times, regardless of money. Goodness is not a shirt you put on in the morning and take off last thing at night. Goodness is something you wear all the time, even in the bath. Like a vest.'

'What happens when the vest is in the wash?' I asked.

'Well you can't wear it then, obviously.'

'So when the vest's in the wash you're bad, are you?'

'Yes,' said Dad, 'definitely. Now fetch us a beer, mate, and I'll give you a fiver.'

I fetched the beer and demanded the fiver, even though Dad called me a 'scrape' and said he hadn't meant it. But the end of the day that was all I had and £5 won't even buy you the back legs of a terrapin. Tomorrow I must earn more before 'Alfred the Mad and Friendless' completely flips his lid and goes on a blood-sucking, poison-pumping, windpipe-wringing rampage.

Mum cooked a special remembrance dinner tonight for the cat Napoleon. There were candles on the table and Dad said a few heartfelt words. Six to be precise.

'Goodbye, Napoleon. You were a cat.' Mel cried and the rest of us looked at the floor.

Vest in wash 150-143

TUESDAY

My big brother is a pig and I am never giving him a birthday present again, unless I have an infectious disease like chickenpox or mumps then I'll give him that! I went to Mum and asked what jobs she had to earn money and she said, 'None, because I've given them to William.'

'But those were *my* jobs!' I gasped. 'And I've got a mad snake upstairs that needs friends!'

William was washing the car before school and when I went to take the sponge off him, he held me at arm's length and counted out imaginary fifty-pound notes under my nose.

'I hope you drink washing-up liquid by accident and choke to death on soapy bubbles!' I said. 'And while you're doing me favours, give me my Cup Final tickets too. I know you've got them!' But instead of answering, he turned the hose on me and I had to go to school in wet trousers like a Second Year. I have probably got pneumonia now – not that anyone cares.

When I got home, my big brother and sister met me in the hall with big grins. They told me that Mum and Michael had had an argument on the phone. They said that the man in charge of the BBC was furious with *me*, because it was my fault that the recording of Mum's cooking couldn't happen till Friday.

Apparently, according to Mel and William, Mum was on the verge of giving me away to an orphanage! I have written the man at the BBC a letter.

Secret Address,
Atrocity Road,
T—ing

Dear Man at the BBC,
Your wife is safe. Do not try to contact us. If you stop saying I was responsible for Mum's cooking programme not being recorded until Friday, she will be returned unharmed.

Love,
A Terrorist.

PS Don't try to find me, because I won't be there.

Before bed, I made Mum a cup of tea and smiled a lot in her direction.

'Are you happier after that tea?' I asked.

'A bit,' she said.

'Oh good. Would you like one of my sweets?'

'I would,' she said. 'What are they?'

'I've forgotten,' I said. 'But they're not very nice.'

'Well I won't then,' she said. Which was just as well, because I didn't have any. I only offered her a sweet to make her like me, and I only wanted her to like me so that I could ask my next question.

'Mummy, if I promise to be good and stay out of your hair for the next few days can I borrow twenty pounds?'

'Only if you practise your piano,' she said.

I walked into that one!

It was torture, but I did it. Only I didn't have to do it for long, because when I played my third note there was that funny squelching noise again and this time there was another noise, a distant screech like a violin played by a chipmunk or Mr E's hideous howling. But it wasn't Mr E.

I opened the lid and discovered a thin and scrawny Napoleon in a corner trying to avoid the hammers as they hit the wires. There was a nasty smell as well. On closer inspection, I discovered to my horror that the piano was full of cat poo, which was why some of the notes had squelched.

Holding Napoleon at arm's length, I entered the sitting room in triumph, fully expecting a hero's welcome. Instead, what I got was abuse from Mel who accused me of deliberately hiding her cat in the piano to upset her.

'If anyone's upset,' I told her, 'it's me. My piano's ruined. The only tune I can play on it now is *Plopsticks*.*'

I mean poor old Mum's set her heart on me having a three-and-a-half-hour lesson this Sunday and now . . .' I turned to Mum with a pained expression on my face,

Move over Brad Pitt, better actor coming through!

'. . . I'm really sorry, Mum, I was sooo looking forward to it . . . but I won't be able to go because I can't practise.'

My mum smiled. 'Talking of which,' she said, 'you assured me that you had been practising, Alistair.'

'Oh yes,' I said warily.

'So how come there was a noisy cat inside the piano pooping on your notes and you never noticed?'

'I think I might be deaf,' I said. 'Like Beethoven.'

'I think you might be lying,' she said. 'Like Pinocchio.'

My punishment was to clean out the inside of my piano with a wet J-cloth and a spoon. After Mum had inspected my work she gave me £20.

'You did find the cat after all,' she said generously. 'But from now on it's an hour's piano practise every day and I shall be watching.'

Could come down to penalties, 150-149

I hope Not

Piano practise before school. Dull and Duller. But *after* school, Aaron, Ralph and me took my £25 to the pet shop and bought a few friends for 'Mad Alfie the

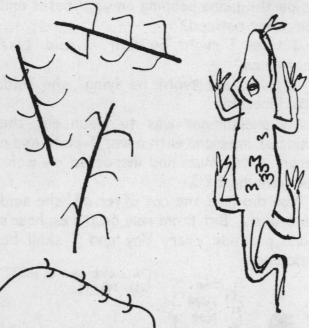

The crickets smirked like they thought they were specially chosen pets, little knowing that they were in fact gecko food!

Snake' – two geckos, six stick insects and an egg box full of crickets!

The geckos are all right to touch, but the stick insects are yucky and sticky with long spindly legs. I only hope that Alfred doesn't hate them as much as I do or he'll never forgive me for rolling him into an anchovy toastie, and if he doesn't forgive me I'm dead in my bed!

'What about some live food for Alfred?' whispered Aaron.

'He'll calm down if he eats.'

'How much are two rats?' I asked the man.

'A pound a tail,' he said.

'Can it be 60p for those two scrawny ones?' I asked. The man took every last penny I had and gave me the two skinny rats. They had mean, shifty eyes and kept touching their mouths with their paws.

'See that,' said Ralph. 'They're lab rats. They're addicted to cigarettes. They need nicotine. I bet they're alcoholics too. I bet

there's nothing they won't do for a drink.'

'Really?' I said. The last thing I needed was two drug-crazed rats nicking money out of Mum's purse to buy cheap cider!

'Got ya!' laughed Ralph. It was his idea of a joke. So I laughed too, but I still didn't like the way those rats were looking at me. The sooner they were Alfred's lunch the happier I'd be.

When I got home, I put the geckos and the stick insects into separate Pyrex casserole dishes and introduced Alfred. 'Geckos and Stick Insects, meet Snake.

Snake, meet Geckos and Stick Insects. You lot can become best mates and play together.' Then I shoved the rats in the cage and introduced them too. 'Snake, Rats. Rats, Snake. Don't get too attached, because he's going to eat you!' At which point Alfred smiled at me and I was forgiven.

Picking up crickets to feed to the geckos is harder than I'd thought. I wasn't going to touch the crickets with my fingers, obviously, so I used Mum's tweezers. Unfortunately I kept tweezing too hard and their legs came off. One of the

↖ stick insects with legs tweezered off (took me ages to draw these!)

crickets actually popped like an over-stuffed pillow.

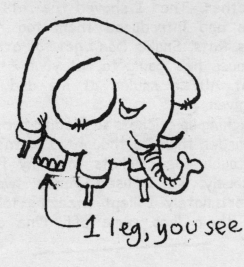

1 leg, you see

More piano practice before bed. *March of The One-Legged Elephant* is the most boring piece of music ever written, employing, as it does, two hundred and sixty three consecutive B flats. Yawn! Yawn! I won't have any trouble sleeping tonight.

My animal army is back to full strength 199-149

THURSDAY

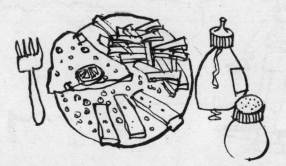

More piano practice. My poor fingers haven't ached so much since William slammed them in the car door.

On the plus side, Mum has stopped cooking for us! Tomorrow, the kitchen is out of bounds, because they're recording the first programme. Michael is very relieved. It's going out on Sunday and they're way behind schedule. Now we can go back to proper food like fish fingers, pizzas and chips!

I received a reply from
the man at the BBC:

Dear Mr Terrorist,
My wife is perfectly safe thank you. She
and I are currently enjoying a lovely break-
fast together in our Victorian-style
conservatory. The sun is shining and the
orange juice is freshly squeezed. In
future, I recommend you heed the famous
words of Omar Khayam; 'He who pulls the
wool over the sheep's eyes must first get
to know the sheep.'
Yours etc

I do not understand a word of this letter, but I shall take it as a full apology and quite right too.

After school, Aaron and Ralph came round to check for themselves that Alfred had stopped being a psychopath.

'He's blooming,' said Ralph, 'but your geckos look peaky.'

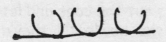

I told him I thought they were hungry.

'And the stickies are shedding their skins,' said Aaron.

It was clear that we had a feeding emergency on our hands. We needed food. Ralph suggested that the Stickies might like a bit of rat.

'Which bit?' I asked. 'The cheek bit, the tail bit or the whiskery bit?'

'The vegetable bit,' said Aaron. 'Stickies are vegetarians.'

'No wonder they're so thin and weedy,' I said. 'Let's raid the kitchen.'

You've never seen so much stuff in one fridge. We took half a dozen bowls each, ran back upstairs and gave the geckos and stickies a slap-up meal. We had no idea what it was, but they seemed to like it. The rats took an interest too. They put their feet on the bars and wiggled their whiskers.

'Go on, give them some,' said Ralph.

'Why?' I said.

'They're on Death Row. Condemned men always get a last meal.'

So we took the rats out the cage and let them run around in the bowls till they'd eaten as much as they could, which was most of everything. In one bowl full of pink mousse and crab claws, they left their little footprints, which was rather sweet. Then we took the bowls downstairs and put them back in the fridge.

After Ralph and Aaron had gone – more piano practice. At this rate I'll have worn out the keyboard by Sunday. I can hear Mrs Muttley's horrible piercing laugh in my head. It is like the whistle of an oncoming train and I am tied to the rails waiting for it to hit me.

It is two o'clock in the morning. The geckos are sleeping on their backs. I have never seen them do this before. The stickies seem OK though, if a little more hyperactive than usual. One stickie has just hurled itself against the glass wall and is lying on its back stunned. It's probably that liver and bacon ice-cream. It has the same effect on me.

One point for crushing the BBC 200-149

FRIDAY

The geckos are obviously having a lie-in, because no amount of banging on their Pyrex dish will wake them. I took the lid off and gave them a poke but neither moved. The stickies have calmed down though, despite overnight leg loss. But the best news is that for the first time in a week, Alfred has lifted his head up and is looking at the rats. He must be hungry, because the rats have started winking and waving back at him, and trying to make best friends so he won't eat them.

More piano. Mum says it's a wonderful skill to possess, that one day I'll thank her when I'm earning money playing piano at the Albert Hall. I didn't realize that *March Of the One-Legged Elephant* was so popular with concert-going audiences.

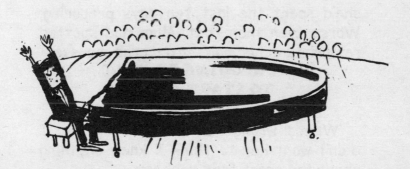

My big brother and sister stopped me at the foot of the stairs. They were both smirking.

'Oh dear, Alice, you're in *such* trouble!' said Mel. 'You might even be sent to live away from home. In an institution with bug-eyed children who wet their beds!' This was the same big sister who'd hung me out of windows when I was four and pointed at police cars. 'They're coming to get you,' she'd said. 'You're going to prison, Alice!' I didn't take any notice of her then and I wasn't taking any notice of her now. But when Napoleon and Mr E suddenly flew out of the kitchen at head height like Superman's cat and dog, I sensed that something was not quite right.

Mum had opened the fridge. Worse than that, Mum had removed the food that she'd spent the last ten days preparing. Worse even than that, Mum had spotted rat-prints in her half-eaten crab mousse.

'I'M GOING TO HAVE TO START AGAIN!'

she wailed.

'What's wrong?' I asked innocently. I didn't want her to think I knew anything about the great food robbery.

'WHAT'S WRONG?'

she shouted.

'What's wrong? I'll tell you what's wrong, Alexander.'

'Alistair,' I whispered, 'but it doesn't matter.'

'SOMEONE HAS EATEN THE FOOD FOR MY PROGRAMME! I'd prepared everything I needed to "prepare earlier" and now somebody's eaten it!'

'It wasn't my pets,' I said. 'I don't know who did it. Maybe it was a burglar.'

'YES! A RAT BURGLAR!'

she roared, shoving the tiny footprints under my nose.

'It wasn't just the rats,' I said before I could stop myself. 'The geckos and stickies ate stuff too! *By accident*!' Suddenly there was a nasty silence.

Then in a slightly shaky voice my mother whispered, 'Get out of my sight. The programme's going to be cancelled. Everything is ruined!'

That was when Michael appeared with the film crew. They had arrived with a van full of equipment and a lorry full of bacon rolls and biscuits. Mum was sitting on the

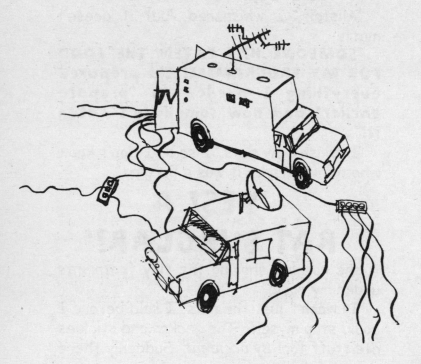

kitchen floor sobbing into a bottle of sherry when William answered the door. 'The patient's in the kitchen,' he said, trying not to smile.

I was in big trouble. I knew that before Michael and Mum staggered out of the kitchen and called us into the hall.

'Children,' she said calmly, 'we will be cooking live!'

'We?' said Mel.

'Because the food has been eaten out of the fridge we cannot record today as planned and I must start again. Tomorrow I will shop and prepare my ingredients. On Sunday, from our kitchen, we will broadcast live to the nation.'

'I still don't get the "we",' said Mel. 'I thought you said it was just *me* who was going to be on telly.'

'If I am to cook live,' said Mum, 'I will need all the help I can get. That means all three of you.' Mel stepped forward to complain, but Mum shut her up by holding the finger-that-must-be-obeyed under her nose.

'Clear Sunday,' she hissed. 'That is all.'

This must be what they mean by every cloud has a silver lining. I do the worst thing I've ever done in my life and my absolutely most awful punishment is to a) get myself back on telly and b) get my

piano lesson cancelled!

March Of The One-Legged Elephant is no more. I have burnt the sheet music in the garden and buried the ashes. This is every Christmas, birthday, skive-off-school day rolled into one. I have never ever been this happy! I am totally full of bliss!

At school, when I told the Revengers about my geckos having a long lie-in, Ralph was rather cold and matter-of-fact. 'They're not kipping,' he said. 'They're dead!

Too much tiramisu!' I said it couldn't be. I was sure I'd seen them move. 'Of course you have,' he said. 'Dead bodies *always* move. It's the maggots!' Aaron asked if he could have a look, because he'd never seen a dead body full of maggots before. I said he could, but he'd have to come early, because I thought tomorrow might be quite a busy day.

Avoided Mum all evening.

A game of two halves - first half 200-250; second half 1493-250III

SATURDAY

Ralph and Aaron rang the doorbell at seven o'clock. Luckily Mum had been up all night so she opened the door and I didn't have to get out of bed.

Aaron and Ralph crouched in front of the geckos' casserole dish for ages, just staring. Then Aaron stood up.

'They're definitely not moving,' he said. 'Have you had a sniff?' I shook my head. So Ralph slid the lid off and we all took one step back.

'Now do you believe me?' Ralph said

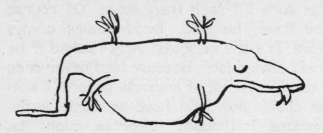

smugly. 'That stink is "dead". "Having a long lie-in" is snoring and stuff.'

'Do you know any hymns?' Aaron asked.

'What for?' I said.

'The funeral.'

'You don't need a funeral for geckos,' Ralph snorted. 'Just feed them to the snake.'

But Alfred turned his nose up at dead gecko and looked hopefully at the rats instead. He liked his meat with a bit of chase in it. But now that I'd got to know the rats I turned squeamish.

'Can't do it,' I said. 'I can't feed him rat. All that blood up the walls. It's too cruel.' Alfred would just have to starve.

When Ralph and Aaron had gone, me, Mel and William were lined up in the kitchen.

'I have to go shopping,' said Mum, 'and I need help.'

'Oh no, I've just remembered,' William said suddenly. 'I'm going to the cinema this morning.'

'Me too!' shouted Mel. 'William and I are going to see that new thing with whatsis-name, you know – actor, hair, does a lot of films.'

'And I'm going too!' I said quickly.*

'No you're not,' smirked William, 'It's a fifteen, Alice, so they won't let you in.'

My mother sighed. 'I'll cut you a deal,' she said. 'If you two big ones could go tonight instead, and take Alistair with you . . .'

'Do we have to?' they groaned.

'I haven't finished!' snapped Mum. 'I will pay. OK? That means I can have some peace to do my cooking.'

'But what about the shopping?' sulked my big brother. 'I'll be too tired to go to the cinema if I've been shopping too.'

'Me too,' whined my big sister. 'And I won't have time to phone my Lukey.'

'Fine!' said my mum sharply. 'Alistair can come shopping with me now, just so long as you two promise to take him off my hands this evening.' *Take him off my hands!* What was I now? A wart?

Shopping was a nightmare. Shopping is *always* a nightmare, because everyone always knows Mum. 'Hello, Celia. What's cooking?' If I had ten pounds for every time I'd heard that, I could buy all the geckos in the world. Inside the supermarket people asked Mum's advice on recipes, or told Mum how their shepherd's pie was nicer than hers, or took things out of our shopping trolley and walked off with them, saying stupid things like, 'Well if it's good enough for Celia Fury it's good enough for me!' For three and a half hours it was nothing but *aisle-aisle-aisle, food-food-food, bored-bored-bored!* But when Mum

my very own cut out and keep 'smile when you're shopping' mask

looked round I made sure it was *smile-smile-smile*, and *happy to be here-happy to be here-happy to be here*, because I didn't want to mess up my big TV break. When we finally got to the checkout some mad,

bearded lady ruffled my hair and said to Mum, 'Ooh, isn't he sweet, Celia! He is yours I take it?'

I stood on tiptoe and whispered in her ear, 'No I'm not. My parents were poisoned to death by one of her prawn recipes and she's had to look after me ever since.' The old lady dropped her eggs and went as pink as the prawns in her basket.

Later that evening, I was 'taken off Mum's hands' by William and Mel and Luke the Puke. From the way Mel had drooled over Luke I was expecting a cross between Brad Pitt and Tom Cruise. In actual fact, with his matted hair and long swinging arms, he looked like an orang-utan and Mel was all over him like a flea.

When we walked down the road towards the cinema they held hands, so I did fart REALLY EMBARRASSING!

noises behind Mel's bottom and he laughed, which made Mel really cross.

'Grow up!' she squeaked. 'Act your age!'

'I am acting my age,' I said. 'I'm eleven. Farts are funny.'

But in the cinema I should have acted older. The film was a '12' and the man in the booth said I was only eight.

'Pants!' I said. 'What are we going to do now that we can't go to the cinema?'

'Wrong!' laughed William. '*You* can't go to the cinema, but *we* can.' Traitors! Hanging was too good for them.

'Don't run out and play with the cars,' said Mel. 'Wait here till we come out.'

'But that won't be for three hours,' I said.

'That's the price you pay for being little!' said William. 'Sit!'

'Don't I even get any chocolate raisins?'

'SIT!' So I sat outside on the cold stone step while they went inside the warm, comfortable, luxury cinema to watch the film.

In the next ten minutes I felt hate, loathing and revenge. Then I nipped round to the fire exit and waited for someone to come out. I slipped inside and found my way into the auditorium. It was dark and the film was loud so nobody knew I was there. I fell to the floor, commando style, and crawled up the aisle on my belly. I could see my big brother with his feet up on the seat in front and my big sister sitting next to him. The boyfriend was at the far end pretending to watch the film, but really taking sneaky looks down Mel's T-shirt.

I crawled between the seats and stopped behind my big brother, then

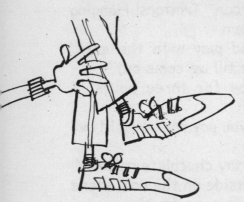

pushed my arm through the gap and stroked his leg. William leapt up with a huge shiver and 'Aagh!' but couldn't see who'd done it.

'What are you doing?' hissed Mel.

'Did you just stroke my leg?' he asked.

'Don't be gross,' she said.

'Sit down!' came a shout from behind. So William sat down.

I gave it three minutes then stuck my hand through another gap and stroked the

boyfriend's leg! Drippy boyfriend only thought it was big sister, didn't he! He stroked her leg back and she slapped him. Whack! Bullseye! He was stunned. He didn't know what had hit him. *Mel Ha ha!*

Meanwhile Mel was sitting there all offended so I crept up behind and slapped *her*. It worked a treat. She thought it was the boyfriend slapping her back and slapped him *again*. Only this time she chucked her Coke and popcorn over him as well. Then she left. It was brilliant. It was like everything I'd planned in my head just happened the way it was meant to.

It was just a shame that William had to see me.

When we got home I had two dead legs and Chinese burns on both my wrists. I tried to explain that it was only a joke, but Mel was in hysterics, because Luke had

139

dumped her, and William had really been enjoying the film when the manager had thrown us out. So basically I had ruined both their lives. Then while Mel bawled in her room, William put my head down the loo. 'You owe me five pounds,' he said.

'What for?' I bubbled.

'For the wasted ticket, Alice.'

'Then you owe me five pounds too,' I said.

'No, I do not.'

'Yes you do!' I shouted, pushing him off

and standing up. 'For all the pain and hardship you've ever caused me. For all the loneliness. For all the times I've tried to be your friend and you wouldn't listen. For leaving me outside the cinema. For stealing my Cup Final tickets. For calling me "little" and that stupid name, "Alice". In short, William Fury, you big pig, you owe me five pounds for being your little brother!' That shut him up.

During supper everyone was quiet. Mum was thinking about recipes, Dad was thinking about the round of golf he couldn't play tomorrow, Mel was crying over lost love and William was watching me.

Afterwards, when we were upstairs, he said, 'You won't ever say what you said to me earlier in front of Mum and Dad, will you?' He was worried I might shop him.

'That depends,' I said. It was fun having all the power! 'That depends on whether you tell me if Cocoa Pops called or not.'

William nodded his head. 'They did,' he said. 'You only came third though, so you've only won one ticket. They said you should pick it up tomorrow from the Wembley box office.'

'Are you serious?' I grinned.

He nodded again. It's a sunny day in Heaven! I knew I'd won. I knew it!

I am the greatest! Me 2,356,223-Them 251

Up early, because the telly people are coming at eight o'clock to set up for tonight's live broadcast. I'm quite nervous, but I bet all the great TV superstars go through the same thing – Les Dennis, Richard Madeley, Keith Chegwin and Orville. It's a humbling thought that when I appear on TV in front of millions I shall be more famous than the Queen!

Michael kept us out of the kitchen all day while Mum rehearsed for the cameras. Dad sat in the living room feeling left out, Mel spent all day in her bedroom doing her make-up, and William and I played Paper, Rock, Scissors and pretended to get on.

At four o'clock we were allowed into the kitchen. We were all excited and Mum was smiling – that fixed smile she does when she's not enjoying birthday parties but pretends that she is.

I won even though he says he let me.

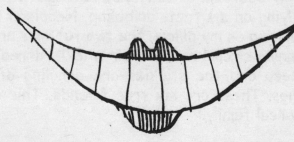

'Right,' she said. 'You know I said you'd all be helping me today . . .' This was the bit I'd been waiting for! 'Well I'm sorry, Alistair, but you're too little.' At first I didn't hear what she said. I mean I heard it, but it didn't seem real. Then it struck home.

'Too little!' I gasped. 'Too little! Why is "little" always so bad? And how can I be too little for telly? Get a smaller camera.'

'It's my fault,' said Michael. 'But the show's live, Alistair, and I can't take the risk that you might mess things up. Mel and William are only handing plates to your mother. They'll hardly be seen at all.' Too little! I was choked. It's not my fault I've got the family's midget gene!

It is 4.30. The show goes on air at 6.30. Everyone except me is downstairs doing a dress rehearsal without food. I am sitting in my bedroom dreaming of revenge. Mr E is lying on my feet, dribbling, Napoleon is moulting on my pillow, the two fat rats are running circles round their wheel, Alfred's asleep and the stickies are dangling off twigs. These are my true friends. This is my real family.

144

5.45 – I've just had a flash.
I phoned up Aaron.

'Peanut butter and jam sandwiches,' I whispered.

'Peanut butter and jam sandwiches.' That was Aaron. 'Speak, fellow Revenger.'

'I need to get my mum back for something horrible she's just done, fellow Revenger.'

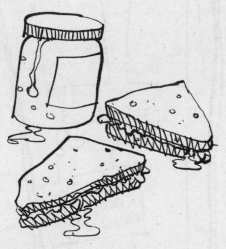

'Hang on, I'll get the other fellow Revenger on the phone too.'

'Is Ralph there?' I asked.

'Ssh!' hissed Aaron. 'No names!'

'Sorry,' I said.

'Peanut butter and jam sandwiches,' said Ralph coming to the phone.

'Peanut butter and jam sandwiches,' I

replied.

'How can I help you, fellow Revenger?' That was Ralph again.

'Like I told Aaron,' I said. 'I've got to get back at my mum big time.'

'That's easy,' said Ralph. 'Strike at the heart!'

'I don't understand,' I said.

'Put these six words in the right order,' said Ralph, 'and you will have your answer. *Programme, cookery, live, the, up* and *mess*.'

'Oh,' I said slyly, cracking the secret code. 'Yes of course!'

6.30 – When Michael called for 'absolute quiet!' and counted down from ten to zero, I crept downstairs with two boxes hidden under my jumper. If I stood on the third step and looked through the glass window above the kitchen door I could see Mum talking to the camera and taking plates of food from my big brother and sister. Mel

was smiling so hard her face was in danger of splitting, and William was trying to look cool by *not* smiling and doing everything dead casual. I could see Dad in the sitting room watching the programme go out live on the telly. He was snoring. Nobody was watching me though, which was just what I wanted.

I crept out the front door, climbed over the back gate and released my weapons through the cat flap. One snake, two rats and six limping stick insects! Then I pressed my nose against

 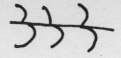

the kitchen window and waited for the fun to begin!

heads explode

glass shatters

Eight million people heard Mel scream when a rat ran up her tights. It was being chased by Napoleon, who'd heard the pitter-patter of tiny rodent feet and had crashed through the cat flap to catch them. Mel fell backwards and knocked her head against a shelf of pots and pans and brought the whole lot crashing to the floor. Michael clamped his hand over her mouth to try and stop her screaming, but a stickie dropped off the ceiling into his

hair, which started him screaming as well. He snatched off his wig and chucked it away, but it landed right in front of Mum, and the stickie fell on the chopping board, where she was showing the nation how to prepare okra. Then while Mel was dragged out and Michael got a good slapping to shut him up, Alfred made his first appearance behind Mum's head. He was hungry now and wanted some rat. He slid over her shoulder and set off after his lunch, knocking all Mum's food off the work surface. He was a good hunter though. He got the rats cornered next to the bread bin, right in front of the camera. Then he wrapped his tail around both rats together, dislocated his jaw and was just about to eat them

whole when two stickies dropped down William's neck. Big brother lost his cool, yelped, whipped off his shirt, and knocked the cameraman off his box. The camera went up in the air and took shots of

the ceiling, while Mum kept on talking as if nothing was wrong. But it was, because when the camera was turned the right way up again, Mum had to show the viewers all her lovely ingredients with her hair crawling with stickies! And behind her Mr E had grabbed Michael's wig in his jaws and was shaking it to death like a rabbit. And behind Mr E, Napoleon and Alfred were locked in a tug of war over the rats, until Alfred's tail lost its grip, the rats tumbled free, Napoleon fell off the counter and the rats, much to every viewer's surprise, ate Alfred. It was quite a rare TV event so I'm told. Nobody had ever seen food eat the eater before, and Napoleon decided not to tangle with the rats after all.

That was when I felt a hand on my collar.
'There you are!' said Michael. 'We've got a problem.'

'I didn't do it!' I said. 'It was an accident. It wasn't me.'

'What are you talking about?' he said. 'I need your help.'

'I thought I was too little,' I said bitterly.

'Not any more,' he said. 'Your brother and sister are too scared to go back into the kitchen while those rats and stick things are in there, and they're meant to be tasting the food at the end of the programme. I need you to do it, Alistair, I need you to walk into that kitchen and save the day!'

'But I hate my mum's food,' I said. 'It

153

makes me sick. I can't pretend to like it.'

'I'm afraid you have to,' said Michael. 'It's called acting.'

But my stomach was starting to feel queasy. 'So what's she cooking?'

'Tooting green curry with lemongrass rice, extra large chilli-balls and a side dish of okra in live yoghurt.'

'What's okra?' I said suspiciously.

'It's green,' said Michael, 'and looks like fingers, but it's covered in yoghurt so you won't see a thing.'

'And if I do this I get to be a television celebrity?'

'Definitely,' he said.

'Then I'll do it,' I said.

I couldn't stop grinning. I grinned at

Michael. I grinned at Mel. I grinned at William. I even grinned at Mum while she talked to the country with a rat on her

shoulder. For the first time in my life I was BIGGER than my brother and sister. I was the chosen one!

I was told to wait behind the camera while Mum finished her cooking. The kitchen looked like a hurricane had just blown through it. There was food and yoghurt and bits of tomato everywhere. Then suddenly everyone was looking at me and Michael pushed me on.

'This is Alexander,' said my mum, 'my littlest.'

'Alistair,' I hissed. How could she get my name wrong with the whole world watching?

'He's going to help me taste what I've cooked. Come and sit beside me,' she said, patting the chair next to her. The camera followed me to the table and stuck its nose in the food I was about to eat. The curry was green, the lemongrass rice had sticks of bamboo in it, and the okra looked like fat twigs in white custard. A plate with everything on was plonked in front of me and I was told to tuck in. I held my breath, put on a smile and started to eat. Surprisingly I didn't mind the taste, although the okras were a bit woody. In fact everything went rather well until, after several forkfuls, something twitched on

my plate. It was one of the okras. It swam through the custard, stood up, lurched forward and hopped across the chilliballs! And just as it did so, my lips were prised open and a thin, sticky leg popped out!

My stomach turned over. My mouth filled with

vmmph

water. I had to remember that I was live on air. I had to remain calm. I had to behave like a TV superstar, but I couldn't! I spat out what was in my mouth and sprayed the camera with yoghurt. Then I looked down at my plate and saw to my horror that what I'd been eating wasn't okra at all. It was a stick insect! My evil mother had cooked my pets! I was a cannibal!

I'm not sticking around there

'I can't keep it down!' I screamed. But my cruel mother ignored my cries and kept smiling.

'And that's all we've got time for,' she said to the nation.

'Here it comes!' My face turned green and I clamped my hand over my mouth.

'Join me again same time next week.'
'MUMMY!'

I'm fed up with this scoring rubbish. It's stupid! I'm not doing it anymore.

'So happy cooking and good . . .' She didn't make it to 'bye', because that was when my mouth erupted in a fountain of pink, orange and green, and eight million people saw what I'd had for breakfast.

This picture was deemed far too gross to be shown. CENSORED

Another early night.
Can't sleep a wink – I can still feel that leg wiggling!

Three men in white coats took Mum off to hospital last night so Dad's taken the week off work to look after us. I think I might be back in Coventry, but nobody will tell me so I don't know for sure.

After school, I took a bus to Wembley Stadium to collect my FA Cup Final ticket, but when I got there nobody knew anything about it – except my big brother of course, who thinks it's the best joke in the world to send me all the way across London to pick up *nothing*! This is war! I have called an  emergency meeting of the Revengers to discuss a plan of action. This time my revenge will be total!

Dad's just called supper, so I'd better go. I shall, however, check that Mr E and Napoleon are safe before I eat a morsel. I shall never get over the shame of belonging to a family that eats its own pets.

Hello, Alice. Big brother and big sister here. You're still downstairs eating supper. Guess what we've just found under your bed. My-oh-my, what a lot of words! Now then, naughty little brother, how shall we make you pay?

Love
M & W

P.S. Remind us - it's Pamela Whitby you love, isn't it?